MISS...

Flame

Have you seen this kitten?

Flame is a magic kitten of royal blood, missing from his own world.
His uncle, Ebony, is very keen that he is found quickly.
Flame may be hard to spot as he often appears in a
variety of fluffy kitten colours but you can recognize him
by his big emerald eyes and whiskers that crackle with magic!

He is believed to be looking for a young friend to take care of him.

Could it be you?

If you find this very special kitten please let Ebony,
ruler of the Lion Throne, know.

Sue Bentley's books for children often include animals or fairies. She lives in Northampton and enjoys reading, going to the cinema, and sitting watching the frogs and newts in her garden pond. If she hadn't been a writer she would probably have been a skydiver or brain surgeon. The main reason she writes is that she can drink pots and pots of tea while she's typing. She has met and owned many cats and each one has brought a special sort of magic to her life.

Magic Kitten

Picture Perfect

SUE BENTLEY

Illustrated by Angela Swan

PUFFIN

To Mowgli — the grey and white scrabbler

PUFFIN BOOKS

Published by the Penguin Group
Penguin Books Ltd, 80 Strand, London WC2R ORL, England
Penguin Group (USA) Inc., 375 Hudson Street, New York, New York 10014, USA
Penguin Group (Canada), 90 Eglinton Avenue East, Suite 700, Toronto, Ontario, Canada M4P 2Y3
(a division of Pearson Penguin Canada Inc.)
Penguin Ireland, 25 St Stephen's Green, Dublin 2, Ireland (a division of Penguin Books Ltd)
Penguin Group (Australia), 250 Camberwell Road, Camberwell, Victoria 3124, Australia
(a division of Pearson Australia Group Pty Ltd)
Penguin Books India Pvt Ltd, 11 Community Centre, Panchsheel Park, New Delhi – 110 017, India
Penguin Group (NZ), 67 Apollo Drive, Rosedale, North Shore 0632, New Zealand
(a division of Pearson New Zealand Ltd)
Penguin Books (South Africa) (Pty) Ltd, 24 Sturdee Avenue, Rosebank, Johannesburg 2196,
South Africa

Penguin Books Ltd, Registered Offices: 80 Strand, London WC2R ORL, England

puffinbooks.com

First published 2008

012

Text copyright © Sue Bentley, 2008
Illustrations copyright © Angela Swan, 2008
All rights reserved

The moral right of the author and illustrator has been asserted

Set in Bembo
Typeset by Palimpsest Book Production Limited, Grangemouth, Stirlingshire
Printed and bound in Great Britain by Clays Ltd, Elcograf S.p.A.

British Library Cataloguing in Publication Data
A CIP catalogue record for this book is available from the British Library

ISBN: 978-0-141-32348-0

www.greenpenguin.co.uk

MIX
Paper from
responsible sources
FSC
www.fsc.org   FSC™ C018179

Penguin Books is committed to a sustainable
future for our business, our readers and our planet.
This book is made from Forest Stewardship
Council™ certified paper.

Prologue

The young white lion brushed against
the tall grasses as he padded down into
the valley. Flame lifted his head,
enjoying the smells of red soil and hot
dusty air. It felt good to be home.

Suddenly a terrifying roar rang out.
'Ebony!'

As a powerful dark shape rose up

from the shadow of some thorn trees, Flame froze. He should have known it wasn't safe to come back. He must find somewhere to hide from his uncle.

A bright flash lit up the valley and a shower of silver sparkles fell where the young white lion had stood. In its place now crouched a tiny, fluffy chocolate-brown kitten. Flame's kitten heart beat fast as he lowered himself on to his belly and crawled behind a fallen tree.

A huge paw, almost as big as Flame was now, reached out of nowhere and scooped the kitten up.

Flame bit back a whine of terror as he was dragged deeper into the tangle of branches. Uncle Ebony had found him! He was finished.

But a kindly face with a scarred muzzle looked down at him. 'Prince Flame. I am glad to see you, but you have returned at a dangerous time,' the old grey lion rumbled.

'Cirrus!' Flame mewed in relief. 'I had hoped that my uncle would be ready to give back the throne he stole from me.'

Cirrus shook his head sadly. 'He will never do that. Ebony wants to rule forever. He has sent many spies to look for you.'

Flame's emerald eyes flashed with anger. 'Then I will fight him now!'

'Bravely said,' Cirrus said, smiling and showing his worn teeth. 'But he is too strong for you. Use this disguise and go back to the other world to hide.

Return when you are stronger and
wiser and then save this land from
Ebony's evil rule.'

Over by the thorn trees, the huge
black lion lifted his head and turned
towards where Cirrus and Flame were
hiding.

'Flame! Come out. Let us finish this!'
Ebony roared. Bunching his muscles he
bounded forward, his mighty paws
thudding against the dry earth.

'Go now, Flame. Save yourself,' Cirrus
urged.

Silver sparks ignited in the tiny
kitten's fluffy chocolate-brown fur.
Flame whined softly as he felt the
power building inside him. He felt
himself falling. Falling . . .

Chapter
ONE

Orla Newton's dad flapped the
newspaper in the air like a fan, so that
it ruffled Orla's short hair.

'Da-ad! Don't! This film's just getting
to the good bit! The aliens are about to
take over the earth!' Orla complained,
glued to the TV screen.

'Judging by all the sci-fi films you

watch, they've already taken over your body!' Mr Newton joked, plonking the paper in her lap.

'Ha ha, very funny!' Orla said, pulling a face as she reluctantly pressed Pause on the DVD controller.

She looked down at the article her dad had circled with black felt tip. 'Wildlife photography competition for local children up to ten years old. Grand prize of a top-of-the-range digital camera and lots of prizes for runners up,' Orla read aloud.

At the mention of a brand-new camera, she felt a flicker of interest.

Mr Newton grinned at the look on his daughter's face. 'Aha! I thought that

would get your attention. Are you
going in for it then?'

Orla shrugged. 'There's no point.
My old camera's useless.'

'No problem. I'll lend you mine,' her
dad said. 'And I can give you a few tips
on taking good snaps.'

'Really?' Orla felt herself starting to
warm to the idea.

'You're going on a school trip to
Borton Pits Nature Reserve on Friday,
aren't you? Sounds like the perfect place
to get some photos,' Mr Newton said
enthusiastically.

'I suppose I could –'

'Guess what? I've been picked for the
county cross-country team!' an excited
voice interrupted.

Orla turned round to see her sister
Grace come bouncing into the sitting
room, her blonde ponytail flying out
behind her.

At twelve, Grace was two years older
than Orla. She practically lived at the
after-school sports club. Orla had been
to it once, but they only seemed
interested in kids who were really good,

so she hadn't bothered going again.

'That's brilliant news! Well done, love.'
Mr Newton came over to give Grace a
hug.

'Yeah. It's great,' Orla said quietly.

Grace pirouetted across the room to
the cabinet that held the silver cups
she'd already won for tennis and
swimming. Straightening her shoulders,
she bent her neck and smiled proudly

as if an invisible judge was looping a medal on a ribbon over her head.

Orla bit back a grin. Grace was such a drama queen! She couldn't help feeling a tiny stir of jealousy, though. It didn't seem fair that her sister was brilliant at every sport she took part in, while she was rubbish.

'Dad? Did you mean it about lending me your camera?' Orla asked on impulse.

'You bet. I'll go and get it right now,' Mr Newton said, smiling as he went into the hall.

'Why do you need to borrow Dad's camera?' Grace asked, frowning.

Orla explained about the wildlife photography competition.

'Huh! You'd better look after Dad's

camera better than you did his posh sunglasses,' Grace said with a chuckle.

Orla felt herself going red. 'I didn't mean to sit on them. It was an accident.'

'Yeah, like when you dropped that cake Mum had just made for Gran's birthday!' Grace reminded her gleefully.

'That wasn't my fault. I tripped over your sports bag that *you* left lying about!' Orla shot back.

'Are you two arguing again?' their mum asked, popping her head round the door.

'No, Mum!' Orla and Grace chorused.

'Hmm.' Mrs Newton didn't look convinced. 'I'm about to make supper. Anyone fancy giving me a hand?'

'Sorry, I can't. Dad's just going to show me how to use his camera,' Orla said quickly. 'But Grace will help, won't you?'

'I don't mind,' Grace said sweetly, but as their mum withdrew her head, she turned and stuck out her tongue at Orla. 'I don't know why you're bothering with this competition! You never stick at anything – except for watching those pathetic films about boggle-eyed aliens!'

'So? They're really good. And I will stick at this. Just watch me!' Orla shot back at her. How hard could it be to point a camera at some dumb old birds and butterflies, after all?

★

On Friday morning, Orla stood in a muddy clearing in Borton Pits, while Miss Bussell divided the class into groups. Two wardens, wearing green jumpers and combat trousers, stood nearby.

'I hope we're not going to be in Bossy Bussell's group,' Joe Manners commented. Joe lived two streets away from Orla and was her best friend in class.

Orla grinned. Miss Bussell was really nice, but she didn't stand for any nonsense – especially from Joe.

One of the wardens came over to Orla's group. 'Hi! I'm Emma. I'll be showing you around,' she said, smiling.

'Great!' Joe said, looking relieved.

'I hope you've all remembered to

bring your cameras,' Emma said, as the group moved off. 'You'll want to get a head start on taking photos with your whole school taking part in this local photography competition. I expect there'll be lots of fantastic entries.'

As Orla fished about in her school bag for her camera, she noticed Joe stuffing his hands into his pockets. 'Where's your camera? Didn't you bring it?' she asked him.

Joe shrugged. 'Yeah, but I can't be bothered with this stupid comp. We've got no chance of winning with ten million other schoolkids going in for it.'

'Don't be a wimp! My dad always says you have to be in it to win it!' Orla teased.

'Who are you calling a wimp?' Joe said indignantly, but he took his camera out.

Orla and Joe followed the others along tree-lined paths. Birdsong filled the air and blue and yellow wild flowers dotted the grass on either side. As they reached the lake, Emma paused and began pointing out interesting ducks and geese.

Orla switched the camera on, trying to remember which setting to turn the dial to. *Dad said to use 'automatic focus'*, she thought, *but which one's that?*

Suddenly there was a loud splashing noise. Two swans seemed to come running across the lake's surface on their black webbed feet, their powerful wings flapping as they prepared for take-off.

'Wow! Look at that!' Joe said, aiming his camera.

All around Orla there were flashes and faint clicks as the other kids took photos of the swans. Orla twiddled the dial in a panic. Just as the swans took off, she raised her camera and pressed the button.

Nothing happened. She'd forgotten to take off the lens cap!

'Wasn't that fantastic? I reckon I got some great shots!' Joe said excitedly.

'I didn't! I missed the whole thing,' Orla said, exasperated. 'That's typical of me. I reckon I need some serious practice with this camera! I'm going over here by myself for a little while.'

'OK. See you later,' Joe said.

Orla pushed through some trees and went down a bank. She found a quiet sunny spot ringed with tall reeds, away from the others. Not far away through the trees, she could hear Emma saying, 'That duck with a wide bill is a shoveller and those others . . .'

Orla spotted a robin on a branch. She quickly aimed the camera and pressed the button, but just captured a blurry shot of the bush as the robin flew away. She had no better luck with a mallard, which decided to dive under just as she took its photograph.

'This really isn't going very well!' she grumbled.

A handsome black and white duck came out of the reeds and began dabbling about. *Third time lucky*, Orla thought, moving closer.

Holding her breath, she crept slowly down the grassy slope towards the duck, but she wasn't looking where she was going and her foot snagged on a bramble catching Orla completely by surprise.

'Oh!' Orla stumbled and the camera slipped from her fingers. It fell to the ground and bounced down the slope. She watched it in horror as it fell into the lake with a faint plopping sound.

'Dad will go bananas!' she groaned. Her heart sank even more as she imagined Grace's gloating face when she heard about the camera disaster.

Suddenly there was a bright flash
and a shower of silver sparks shot over
Orla's head into the lake. To her
amazement, the camera slowly rose up
out of the water, floated back through
the air and landed in her waiting hands!

Chapter
★ TWO ★

Orla clutched the camera in numb fingers, trying to make sense of what had just happened.

'I hope that I was in time to stop your little silver box from being damaged,' mewed a tiny voice.

Orla whipped round in surprise. 'Who's there? Who said that?'

'I did,' answered the same voice.

Orla looked up the grassy slope and saw a tiny, fluffy chocolate-brown kitten with bright emerald eyes sitting on a nearby log. Its fur glittered in the sunlight, as if it was dotted with hundreds of tiny diamonds.

Orla gazed at the kitten in complete amazement. 'D–did you just answer me?'

The kitten nodded. 'My name is
Prince Flame. What is yours?'

'I-I'm Orla Newton,' Orla stammered.

The kitten pricked its tiny brown
ears. 'I am pleased to meet you, Orla.
I have come from far away.'

'Wow! Are you from another galaxy?'
Orla asked, excitedly thinking of all her
sci-fi films. 'I bet a horrible alien from
the planet Zarg or somewhere is after
you!'

'I do not know of these aliens.'
Flame's brown whiskers began to
tremble with fear. 'But I am in danger.
My Uncle Ebony sends his spies to find
me. He wants to keep the Lion Throne
he stole from me.'

Orla blinked at Flame. Now that the

weird sparkles in his coat seemed to
have died down, Flame certainly looked
like an earth cat. In fact, with his fluffy
rich-brown fur, huge green eyes and
alert pricked ears, Flame was the most
gorgeous kitten she had ever seen.

She felt a surge of protectiveness
towards him. 'Lion Throne? Don't
you mean Kitten Throne?' she asked
gently.

'I will show you!' Flame lifted his tiny
head proudly and there was another
bright silver flash and a spray of sparks
as he jumped off the log.

'Oh!' Orla blinked, blinded for a
moment. When she could see again, she
saw that the tiny brown kitten had
vanished, but in its place stood a

magnificent young white lion. Tiny
points of light like a million rainbows
glittered in its thick velvety fur.

'Flame?' Orla gasped, eyeing the lion's
huge teeth and sharp claws. She stepped
back hastily.

'Yes, Orla. It is me. Do not be afraid,'
Flame answered in a deep gentle growl.

Before Orla could get used to the
regal young lion, there was a final silver
flash and the fluffy chocolate-brown
kitten stood there in its place once
more.

'Wow! You really are a lion prince.
That's so cool!' Orla exclaimed.

Flame blinked up at her again and
she saw that his tiny kitten body was
beginning to tremble with fear again.

'I must find somewhere to hide. Will you help me, Orla?'

Orla's heart went out to Flame. As a young white lion he was scary and impressive, but as a kitten he was adorable. 'Of course I will! I'll take you home with me,' she said, bending down and picking him up.

Flame began purring softly as she stroked his fluffy little head.

There was a rustling sound behind Orla. Flame tensed against her as someone pushed through the trees.

'I bet it's only Joe. He's my friend. He's going to be *so* surprised when I tell him about you!' Orla said excitedly.

'No! No one must know my secret,'

Flame told her, his face serious. 'You
must promise me.'

Orla felt disappointed that she
couldn't share her marvellous discovery
with Joe, but if it helped to keep Flame
safe she was willing to agree. 'All right.
Cross my heart.'

Seconds later Joe appeared. 'Did you manage to get your camera to work?' he said, and then his eyes widened as he saw Flame. 'Where did you get that kitten from?'

'I've just found him. He told me he's called Fla–' Orla stopped hastily, realizing that she was going to have to be a lot more careful about keeping Flame's secret. 'I mean I've decided to call him Flame,' she went on. 'We're miles away from any houses here, so he must be a stray. I'm taking him home to live with me.'

Joe reached out to stroke Flame's ears. 'Aw, he's dead cute. I like his name. If your parents won't let you keep Flame, I'll have him.'

'Sorry, no chance!' Orla held Flame close protectively.

Joe grinned. 'Fair enough. Finders keepers.' He frowned suddenly. 'You'll never get Flame past Bossy Bussell. She's got eyes in the back of her head.'

Orla thought hard. 'I'll hide him in my school bag. He's going to have to stay very still and quiet until school ends, aren't you?' she said gently, looking meaningfully at Flame as she opened her bag.

Flame gave a tiny nod. He jumped straight inside her bag and curled up next to her schoolbooks.

'That's one smart kitten,' Joe said admiringly. 'It's like he knew what you just said.'

Orla bit back a grin. If only Joe knew!

'Bye. Have a good weekend!' Orla called to Joe after school, as she left him at the end of her road.

'We're going off to visit my nan as soon as I get home, so I'll call for you before school on Monday,' he called back. 'Take good care of Flame!'

'I will!'

Orla held her school bag in her arms so she wouldn't jostle Flame as she walked up to her house and went inside. 'Hi! I'm home,' she called.

'Hi.' Grace was sitting at the kitchen table with a glass of milk and some biscuits. She was reading a sports magazine and didn't look up as Orla came in.

'Where's Mum?' Orla asked.

'On her way back from the shops by now,' Grace said, munching.

'Grace, I've got something to show you.' Orla lifted Flame out of her bag and cradled him in her arms. 'This is Flame.'

'What?' Grace glanced up with
a bored expression, but her face
immediately changed as soon as she saw
Flame. 'He's so cute! Whose is he?' she
crooned, rubbing Flame under his chin.

'Mine,' Orla said proudly. 'He's a stray.
I found him and he's going to live here
with me.'

Grace's smile faded. 'No way!
Remember when I wanted a puppy last
year? Mum and Dad said it wasn't fair
to have one cos we're all out all day.
That goes for kittens too!'

Orla felt her heart sink as she realized
that Grace was right. She carefully put
Flame back in her bag, before
shouldering it again and going into
the hall. 'I'm just going back out for a

minute. I won't be long,' she called.

'Where are you going?' Grace called back suspiciously, but Orla was already closing the front door.

Orla wracked her brains as she walked back down the street. There was no way she was going to abandon Flame. 'I can't take you over to Joe's, even if I wanted to. He'll have gone to his nan's by now. And now Grace knows about you, I can't hide you in my bedroom,' she told Flame miserably.

Flame blinked at her from inside her bag. 'But I can hide myself. I will use my magic so that no one except you will be able to see and hear me.'

'Really? You can make yourself invisible?' Orla stopped in her tracks.

'That's fantastic. So you *can* live with me and no one need ever know – not even Grace. Yay!'

She hurried back towards her house. As she came in, she found her mum in the kitchen unpacking the shopping. Grace was helping to put stuff away.

'I've just been telling Mum about *your* kitten,' Grace said straight away.

'What kitten?' Orla said innocently.

Grace scowled at her. 'Duh! That one you just brought in and told me you were keeping!'

'Now, Orla? You know how we feel about having pets . . .' her mum said firmly.

'I know. It was, um . . . a joke about me keeping him . . .' Orla faltered and

then she had a sudden brainwave.
'Flame really belongs to Joe Manners.
I've just taken him back over there. I
was just playing a trick on Grace!' she
fibbed, heading straight for the stairs
before anyone asked any awkward
questions. 'I'm going up to do my
homework now!'

Grace followed her to the bottom of the stairs. 'You made me look a right nit. You rotten little squirt!'

'Serves you right for telling tales!' Orla said, giggling.

In her bedroom, she made a cosy nest for Flame on her duvet. 'There, you're safe now. Even if Grace phones Joe's house to check up on me, she won't get any answer! I'm so glad you're going to live with me,' she told him.

'I am glad too,' Flame gave an extra loud purr and began pedalling the duvet with his tiny brown front paws.

Chapter
★ THREE ★

'How did you get on at Borton Pits?'
Mr Newton asked later as Orla came
back downstairs after smuggling a piece
of fish from supper up to Flame.

'It was OK,' she replied. 'A nice warden
called Emma showed us around. We saw
lots of ducks and stuff.'

'Let's have a look at your photos then.

Did you manage to remember what I told you about zooming in and getting things in focus?'

'Not exactly. I got a bit muddled up,' Orla admitted. She went to fetch the camera. 'The photos aren't very good. I need a lot more practice . . .' she began reluctantly as she walked back into the sitting room with the camera.

Grace lunged forward and snatched it out of her hands. 'Let's have a look!' she said, skipping across the room and plonking herself down next to her dad.

Orla wandered slowly over. She stood behind the sofa, watching over their shoulders as her dad scrolled through her photos.

'Oh look, it's a mega-boring old
bush!' Grace shrieked, pointing to the
screen. 'And a bit of lake! I think I
might faint with excitement!'

Orla bit her lip, feeling her face grow
hot. There were only two photos and
they were both terrible. But she could
hardly explain that after finding Flame,
she'd been too excited to take any
better ones.

'Orla can't take a good photo for toffee!' Grace jeered.

Orla put her hands on her hips. 'Maybe *you* should go in for the photo comp, instead. You're the one with all the talent around here!'

'Simmer down, you two,' Mr Newton said mildly. 'Don't worry, Orla. It takes a while to get used to a new camera.' He got up and went towards the door. 'I've got you something that might give you some ideas. I popped into Andy and Bex's house on the way home from work.'

Uncle Andy and Auntie Bex were Orla's favourite relatives. They were dead keen on wildlife and had a huge garden with a wild flower meadow, a pond and dozens of bird feeders.

Her dad returned with a pile of wildlife magazines. 'There you go,' he said, handing them to her.

Orla gave him a hug. 'Thanks, Dad! These are brilliant. I'll go up to my room and have a look at them, right now!'

'As if *that's* going to make any difference,' Grace murmured.

Mrs Newton came in, jangling her car keys. 'Ready for sports club, Grace?'

'Just coming!' Grace picked up her smart sports bag and swept out of the room. 'Laters, everyone!' she called over her shoulder.

Orla didn't answer her. She ran upstairs to find Flame sitting on her rug, licking his lips after finishing his supper. Orla threw herself down beside him and began leafing through the magazines.

'Some of these photos are brilliant. Look at this one, Flame,' she said, showing him a picture of a wood mouse.

Flame pricked his ears. His tail twitched excitedly and he jumped on to the page, dabbing at the mouse with a tiny front paw.

Orla giggled. 'It looks almost real, doesn't it? Look at this sunset and this close-up of a red poppy! I didn't realize that ordinary things could look so special.' She sat up as an idea came into her head. 'Come on! We're going out.'

As Orla jumped to her feet, Flame tilted his head. 'Where are we going?'

'To ask Dad if I can go to the park. I'm going to have a *proper* go at taking photos!'

★

As Orla walked the short distance to the nearby park, Flame trotted along at her heels invisible to everyone except her.

It was a warm evening. There were people walking dogs in the park and some boys playing football. Four girls who looked about twelve years old were hanging about around the children's playground.

Orla was ready with her camera this time. She looked around for something to photograph and immediately spotted a squirrel near some trees.

Flame had seen it too. He froze in a crouch and his bottom wriggled excitedly as he got ready to spring at it.

'No! Don't chase it, Flame! I want

to take its photo,' Orla whispered
urgently.

Flame gave a soft mew of
disappointment, but lay down
obediently. Orla aimed the camera at
the squirrel and started to press the
button slowly. But the squirrel was wary
of Flame. It bounded across the grass
and shot straight up a tree.

'I don't think I got it. Never mind.
I'll try a few unusual close-ups, like
in those magazines,' Orla decided. She
took a few photos of daises and clover,
but somehow she couldn't seem to get
inspired by flowers.

As she straightened up, she noticed
that the four older girls from the kids'
playground were coming towards her.

The tallest of them, a blonde girl, was only a few metres away now. 'Give us a go with your camera!' she called.

'Sorry, I can't. It's my dad's,' Orla said.

'So what? He isn't going to know, is he?' said another girl.

'Yeah! So give us a go with it, or we'll help ourselves!' called the blonde girl.

Orla's tummy lurched. The girls all looked tough and they were a lot bigger than her. She wasn't going to stay and argue with them.

'I've got to go now!' she called out, stuffing the camera into her shoulder bag. 'Come on!' she said urgently to Flame.

'Hey! Come back!' Orla heard
pounding feet behind her as the older
girls gave chase.

Orla and Flame tore across the park.

Flame started to fall back behind
Orla. He was running flat out, but his
tiny legs couldn't keep up. Orla stopped
and went back for him. Picking him up,
she started running again, but she'd lost
time and she couldn't run as fast with
Flame clutched to her chest.

The older girls were gaining on her.

There was a thick clump of oak trees
some distance away at the back of the
park. Orla put on a spurt and quickly
veered towards them. Gasping for
breath, she reached the trees and rushed
behind one of their thick trunks.

Seconds later, she heard leaves
crunching as the four girls crashed in
after her.

Suddenly Orla felt a warm prickling
feeling down her spine. Her palms
fizzed gently as bright sparks ignited in

Flame's chocolate-brown fur and his whiskers crackled with electricity.

Something strange was about to happen!

Chapter
★ FOUR ★

Time seemed to stand still.

Silver sparks swirled around Orla
and Flame, spinning faster and faster,
until it seemed as if they stood inside
a glittering Christmas snow dome.

Orla's whole body tingled and her
arms and legs felt all light and wobbly.
A blur of brown trunk and leafy

branches whooshed past her.

Orla blinked. She seemed to be sitting on a branch, metres and metres up, high at the top of one of the oak trees. All around were thick branches with big oak leaves.

Orla gulped hard and clung on tightly.

'I won't let you fall,' Flame mewed, crouched on a smaller branch next to her.

Down on the ground Orla could see the tops of the girls' heads as they checked behind each tree for her.

'Where's she gone?' Orla heard the blonde girl ask in frustration. The others stood scratching their heads and looking puzzled.

Orla forgot her fear of being so high
up and stifled a giggle. *This is amazing*,
she thought.

Looking out, she could see the whole
park – people walking their dogs, the
football game still going on and
children playing on the swings.

Another cloud of sparks whizzed
round her and there was a rushing
sensation. Orla found herself on the

grass at the opposite side of the park.
She looked down at the fluffy
chocolate-brown kitten, rubbing
himself against her ankles.

'Wow! That was amazing, Flame!
I *loved* being up that high!' she said,
picking him up and cuddling him.
'Those mean girls were totally confused.
Thanks so much.'

'You are welcome. I am glad I was
able to help,' Flame purred happily.
'Thank you for coming back for me,
when I could not keep up with you.'

'I'd never let anyone hurt you, Flame!'
Orla told him. 'But we'd better go
straight home. I don't fancy bumping
into them again. I can walk more
quickly if you get in my bag.'

Flame nodded. He jumped inside and then poked his head out of the open zip to look around as Orla set off and hurried home.

'Any luck taking pics in the park, love?' Mrs Newton asked as Orla came into the sitting room.

She was back from dropping Grace at sports club and was watching her favourite quiz show on TV. Mr Newton was reading a newspaper. He looked over and raised his eyebrows in a silent question.

'Not really, but it was good practice,' Orla told them casually.

She hid a smile, imagining her parents' look of shocked amazement if

she told them about balancing at the
very top of one of the enormous old
oak trees. 'I think I'll make some hot
chocolate and go up to my bedroom.
I'm going to read a bit before bed.
Anyone else want a hot drink?'

'No thanks, love. We've just had one,'
her mum said. 'I'll pop up and say
goodnight to you later.'

In the kitchen, Orla made the hot
chocolate. She poured some milk for
Flame and took it upstairs with her.
He lapped it up with his little pink
tongue, purring with enjoyment, before
jumping on her bed and curling up
next to her.

Orla stroked his soft fur as she looked
through some more magazines. 'I love

having you living here with me,' she
told him fondly.

Flame looked up at her. His eyes
were narrow slits of contentment. 'I feel
safe with you, Orla,' he said with an
extra big purr.

Orla was just finishing putting on her
school uniform on Monday morning.
'Now, you'll be fine staying in my
bedroom while I'm at −' she stopped as
she saw that Flame was already sitting
inside her open school bag, an
expectant grin on his furry little face.

'OK. I get the message!' she said,
trying not to laugh. He looked so cute
and mischievous sitting there with just
the tips of his sharp little teeth showing.

'Are you sure about this? There'll be loads of kids around. You could get into all kinds of trouble.'

'Do not worry about me. Only you will be able to see me,' Flame reminded her.

'Well, all right then,' Orla agreed. Having Flame with her would make school heaps more fun.

The doorbell rang.

'Joe's here,' her mum called up the stairs.

'Thanks, Mum. See you later!' Orla cried, going downstairs to meet him. 'How was your grandma?' she asked Joe as they set off for school.

'Great. She's loads of fun and a brilliant cook. What happened with Flame? Did your mum and dad let you keep him?' Joe asked eagerly.

'Not exactly. I . . . um . . . told them he belonged to you,' Orla admitted.

Joe's eyes widened. 'What did you do that for?'

'I had to think of something quickly if I wanted to keep Flame without my parents knowing. I'd already shown him to Grace. And you know what she's like for blabbing . . .' she stopped, seeing that Joe looked confused. 'Look. All you need to know is that everyone *thinks* Flame lives with you, but he *really* lives with me. I'm hiding him in my bedroom.'

Joe's face cleared. 'Cool!' he said admiringly.

'If Grace ever mentions a kitten just remember that you're supposed to be Flame's owner,' Orla said. *This is starting to get very complicated*, she thought.

She didn't like telling fibs and was useless at it anyway, as she usually forgot what she'd said in the first place. But there was really no choice if she was going to keep Flame safe from his enemies.

In class Miss Bussell finished taking the register. 'OK, everyone, nature books out, please. We're going to carry on with our work on British wildlife. I'd like you to start working through exercise four on page thirteen.'

As Orla opened her bag, Flame jumped out. He leapt silently and invisibly up on to her desk and then sat there washing his face. Orla smiled. It was still strange to get used to having Flame in full view while knowing that no one else could see him.

Orla glanced up from her workbook to see that Miss Bussell had finished

clearing a big noticeboard. She was
pinning up a sign, which read 'Our
Wildlife Photographs'.

'After break, we'll start pinning up
your photos. I hope you've all
remembered to bring some,' Miss
Bussell said.

'I didn't know we had to!' Orla
whispered to Joe.

'She told us on the coach back to

school after we'd been to Borton Pits,'
he replied.

'Did she?' Orla realized that she must
have been too nervous about making
sure that no one saw Flame to take any
notice.

Flame came over and jumped into
Orla's lap. 'Is something wrong?' he
mewed worriedly.

She stroked him under her desk.
'I was supposed to bring some photos
with me for the noticeboard.' She bit
her lip. 'I don't seem to be able to get
anything right lately.'

'That is not true. You are a very good
friend,' Flame purred indignantly.

'Thanks, Flame,' Orla said, feeling a
bit better.

As the bell went for break, Orla sighed. 'Anyway. Let's go over to the playing fields. I'd bet you'd love a run about,' she whispered to Flame.

As Flame scampered outside after her, Orla didn't notice the thoughtful gleam in his eyes.

Chapter
★FIVE★

As Orla entered the classroom after
break ended, she heard loud whoops
of laughter from a few kids near the
noticeboard.

Flame picked up his paws and held
his head high, looking very pleased
with himself as he ran across the room
ahead of Orla.

'What's going on?' Orla wondered
and then she gasped as she saw the
noticeboard.

The whole thing was covered by a
poster-sized picture. It was a blown-up,
not very good photo of a lot of grass,
with a tiny, startled-looking squirrel in
the bottom corner. Next to it, a neat
card read 'Orla Newton. Squirrel in the
Park'.

'But? How? When?' Orla stammered
and then the penny dropped. 'Flame!'
She looked over towards where he was,
beaming proudly at her from the top of
a bookcase.

'Couldn't you have found a bigger
photo?' one of Orla's classmates
commented.

'Or a decent one anyway!' another of
them said, giggling.

'It was *meant* to be a joke!' Orla said
quickly, going over to take it down.
Rolling it up, she thrust it into her bag
just as the rest of the class and Miss
Bussell came in.

'Quiet, please!' the teacher said,

clapping her hands. 'I'd like you all to get your photos out now and we'll start putting them up.'

Orla sidled to the back of the room, wishing like mad that she was invisible like Flame.

She heard a tiny thud as Flame jumped to the floor and came running over.

'Did I do something wrong?' he mewed worriedly.

Orla glanced down at him. 'It's OK, I know you were trying to help. But I think you'd best leave the photo stuff to me, otherwise it's cheating,' she whispered.

Flame nodded. 'I understand.'

Orla watched enviously as kids began

putting up their photos. There were
some really good ones of ducks and
swans and some of birds on feeders
and frogs in ponds.

Joe was one of the last to go over
to the board. He looked over and
winked at Orla as he pinned his photo
up.

Orla frowned. What was Joe up to?
She watched as he pinned up a photo
– of a bare foot!

'Orla? Did you bring –' Miss Bussell
stopped as she caught sight of Joe's
photo. 'Joseph Manners! Your foot's
hardly wildlife, is it?' she said sternly.

'It *is*, Miss!' Joe paused for effect. 'I've
got athlete's foot and Mum says it's a
fungus – just like mushrooms!'

Orla cracked up laughing. The whole class joined in and even Miss Bussell looked as if she was having a job keeping a straight face.

'That is *so* gross!' Orla spluttered.

Miss Bussell clapped her hands for quiet. 'Very funny. But acting the fool won't win you any prizes. You can take that photo down now, Joe!'

'Yes, Miss,' Joe said.

'Phew! That was a lucky escape,' Orla whispered to Flame as normal lessons started. 'Thanks to Joe, Miss Bussell seems to have forgotten all about me and I won't get told off for forgetting my photos. But I've got to get some good pics soon or I've got no chance of winning that posh camera. There's only a week left to hand your photos in.'

The following Saturday afternoon, Orla sighed as she looked out at the rain-blurred street. 'I was hoping we could go out, but I suppose we could always watch some of my *Battlestar Galactica* tapes,' she commented.

Flame didn't answer. He was standing up on his back legs on the window sill, snapping at a raindrop that was trickling down the glass.

Orla smiled. It was sometimes hard to remember that Flame was a majestic young white lion in disguise.

She reached out to stroke the tiny kitten's little fluffy brown head. 'I wish you could live here with me forever.'

Flame sat down and turned to face her. 'I will stay as long as I can, but one day I must return to my own world and take back my throne. Do you understand that, Orla?' he mewed gently, his green eyes serious.

Orla nodded, but she didn't want to think about that now.

She leaned forward and looked out of
the window. 'Hey! It's stopped raining.
We can go out and find some good
stuff to photograph!'

Flame leapt from the window sill on
to her bed and landed on some of the
wildlife magazines from her aunt and
uncle. With a startled mew, he skidded
straight across the glossy covers, fell off

the bed and plopped on to the soft
bedside rug.

'Oops! Are you OK?' Orla said, trying
not to laugh and hurt his feelings.

Flame shook out his ruffled fur. 'I am
fine,' he purred, trying to sound
dignified.

As Orla picked up the magazines to
put them away, she had an idea. 'I know
where we can go: Uncle Andy and
Auntie Bex's house! They've got a
brilliant wildlife garden. I'm going to
phone them right now!'

Orla's aunt and uncle were delighted to
hear from her and invited her straight
over.

She went outside to tell her dad.

Mr Newton looked up from washing his car. 'I'm popping out in a minute to collect Grace from running club. I can drop you off there if you like,' he offered.

'No. It's OK, thanks. I'll walk over,' Orla said. She thought Flame would enjoy some fresh air.

She set off with Flame scampering along at her heels. They went in the direction of the park and then turned down a side street. A big road full of shops ran along the bottom. Her aunt and uncle lived in a road that led off that.

Orla slowed down as she and Flame reached the road with all the shops. 'I think I'll stop and get a drink and some crisps,' she said, fishing in her jeans for her pocket money.

Four familiar figures came out of the newsagent's as Orla approached.

It was the mean girls from the park.

Orla hesitated. But it was too late to turn back. The girls had seen her.

Chapter
★ SIX ★

'Well, if it isn't that snotty kid with the camera,' the tall blonde girl who seemed to be the ringleader sneered.

'Look! She's got a kitten with her this time!' another of the girls said, pointing at Flame.

Orla's heart missed a beat. They could

see Flame! He must have forgotten to stay invisible.

The blonde girl came right up to Orla. She stood in front of her with her hands on her hips, blocking the pavement. 'Hand over that camera,' she ordered.

'I c-can't,' Orla stammered nervously. 'It's not mine.'

'OK then. I'll have this instead! I fancy a new pet!' Before Orla realized what was happening the blonde girl bent down and grabbed Flame in both hands.

Flame mewed with shock and tried to wriggle free, but the girl tightened her hands round his middle.

'Hold still, you little fleabag!' she ordered crossly.

Flame whimpered with pain and lashed his tail.

Orla lunged forward. She grabbed the bigger girl's hands and tried to prise Flame free. 'Give him back! You're hurting him!'

'Hey! Get off her, you muppet!' One of the other girls gave Orla a shove.

'Oh!' Orla lost her balance and stumbled against a wall.

She banged her knee hard, but she

hardly noticed the pain. Her mind was racing as she tried desperately to think of a way to get Flame back. She'd just have to give them her dad's camera, but then she remembered her pocket money.

She held out a handful of coins. 'Give me Flame back and I'll give you this!'

The blonde girl looked undecided and then she thrust Flame at Orla. 'Here, have the mangy fleabag.' Grabbing the money, she smirked as she and her friends walked away.

Orla cradled Flame against her T-shirt as the girls went into a shop further down the road. She could feel him trembling and his tiny heart was beating fast against her hand. 'It's OK. You're

safe now. Come on, let's go before
those horrible girls come back out.'

'Ow!' Orla gasped at the sudden
sharp pain in her knee. Biting back
tears, she limped into a side street.

Flame leaned up to put his front paws
round her neck. 'Thank you, Orla. You
were very brave. But you are hurt,' he
said, blinking in concern. 'Quick. Take
me into that alleyway.'

Orla did as Flame asked. She held on
to the wall to steady herself.

As soon as they were alone, she felt
the familiar warm prickling sensation
down her back as silver sparks ignited
in Flame's chocolate-brown fur. He
pointed a tiny paw and a fountain of
soft pink sparks shot towards her knee.

The pain increased for a second and
then Orla felt it draining away, just as if
someone had poured it out on to the
ground.

'Thanks, Flame! My knee's fine now,'
she said, kissing the top of his fluffy
head.

'You are welcome,' Flame purred.

'Don't forget to stay invisible from now on, will you? Especially when we're with my aunt and uncle,' Orla reminded him.

'Orla! Come on in,' Andy Newton said, opening the front door ten minutes later. 'Are you all by yourself?'

'Yes, we . . . I mean . . . I walked,' she told her uncle as she followed him into the house with Flame in her shoulder bag.

Uncle Andy looked at her closely. 'Are you all right, love? You look a bit pale.'

Orla realized that she still felt a bit wobbly after the encounter with the older girls. 'I'm, er . . . just thirsty. Can I have a drink, please?' she said.

'Course you can. Come into the kitchen. I'll get you one out of the fridge.'

Orla wandered in after him. She put her bag down, so Flame could jump out.

'Where's Auntie Bex?' she asked.

'In the garden. Why don't you go on out and say hello to her?' Uncle Andy suggested. 'I'll bring some cool drinks out for all of us.'

'OK, thanks.' Orla slid open the big patio doors and Flame followed her outside. 'You're going to *love* exploring this garden,' she said as they passed tubs of bright orange flowers and clumps of scented herbs.

Orla started walking across the enormous lawn, which was dotted with purple clover. As a butterfly fluttered up from one of the flowers, Flame gave an eager mew and darted after it. Orla smiled and left him to enjoy himself.

'Hi, Auntie Bex!' she called to her aunt who was standing at the far end of the lawn near a very complicated structure.

It had poles of differing heights, some topped with little wooden platforms or tiny houses. Loops of rope were strung

between the poles, linking them into a circle. It was a bird feeding station, Orla realized. She was sure it hadn't been there the last time she'd visited.

'Hello, love.' Bex Newton smiled at her niece. 'I'm just filling up these feeders. Do you want to give me a hand?'

'OK.' Orla helped to hang up some strings of peanuts. 'That's a dead posh feeder. You must get zillions of birds in your garden!' she said.

Auntie Bex grinned. 'Maybe not *quite* that many, but we do get lots. Sparrows, blue-tits, wrens and all sorts of finches. Your uncle has just made this new feeding station, but it isn't for the birds.'

Orla frowned. 'What's it for then?'

'For something really unusual that's only been visiting our garden for a week or so and has been pinching the birds' food!' her aunt said mysteriously. 'This is an experiment. We thought if we made something especially for our new visitors, they might leave the other feeders alone.'

'And is it working?' Orla asked, intrigued.

'I hope you'll be able to see for yourself. They usually visit about this time in the afternoon,' said Auntie Bex.

'Really?' Orla's imagination began working overtime. What could the unusual visitors be? 'Is it something that's escaped from a zoo?' she asked.

Sitting over by the table, Uncle Andy laughed. 'I don't think so. But you can judge for yourself. Here they come now.'

'Look at the plum tree, Orla,' her aunt said softly.

Orla saw two slim, dark shapes weaving expertly through the branches. They ran down the trunk, dropped to the grass and bounded across to the feeding station.

Orla watched delightedly, taking in every detail of the alert bright eyes, tiny hands and bushy tails. They were squirrels. But she had never seen anything like them.

From the tufted tips of their ears to the ends of their tails they were a glossy coal-black!

Chapter
★ SEVEN ★

'Wow! They're *so* amazing!' Orla
breathed, watching the black squirrels
on the feeding station.

They were experts at shinning up
and down the poles and snaking across
the drooping ropes. One by one, they
leapt on to the tiny platforms and
reached inside the little carved houses,

helping themselves to tasty snacks.

'Aren't they?' Uncle Andy agreed.
'We've been watching them performing
their acrobatics on that feeder for the
last week or so. They've got quite used
to us sitting here.'

'I thought squirrels were always grey
or red. Why are these ones black?' Orla
wanted to know.

'We don't really know. But we think it's something to do with genetics. We once had a blackbird with white wing feathers in the garden,' her aunt said.

Orla nodded. She had done genetics in science and she had seen albino mice and rabbits with white fur and pink eyes.

'I'm going to take a photo of the black squirrels,' she said. Very slowly, so she didn't make any sudden movements, Orla reached down beside her chair for her bag. But then she remembered that she'd left it in the kitchen. 'Oh no. My camera's inside my bag. If I get up to fetch it the squirrels will run away, won't they?'

'Probably, but don't worry,' Auntie

Bex said. 'They come here every day at about the same time. Why don't you come back tomorrow afternoon?'

'You could come a bit earlier and get organized,' her uncle suggested. 'If you hide yourself over there you'll be able to get some really good close-ups,' he said, pointing to a bush with big pink flowers.

'That's a great idea!' Orla said, beaming. She couldn't wait to come back and take some photos of the unusual black squirrels.

Flame came bounding across the lawn and curled up under Orla's chair as her aunt was bringing out the tea. The home-made cheese scones and chocolate cake were delicious. Orla managed to drop a few cheesy crumbs on the grass for Flame without anyone noticing.

After tea, her aunt and uncle offered to drive her home.

'Thanks very much,' Orla said gratefully. She didn't mind walking but she didn't fancy bumping into those girls again, especially after how they'd treated Flame.

As they drove back past the park, Orla saw a police car parked near the gates. Two policemen stood on the pavement beside a familiar group of four girls. A smaller girl stood there, looking upset and a woman, who looked like her mother, was pointing at the four girls and shouting angrily.

'It looks like someone's in trouble,'
Uncle Andy said, glancing at Orla in
the driver's mirror. 'Do you know those
girls?'

'Kind of, but not very well,' Orla
replied from the back seat. She
lowered her voice and whispered to
Flame who was sitting on her lap. 'I
reckon they've been up to their mean
tricks again and the girl's mum's
reported them this time. Serves them

right. Maybe they'll stop picking on smaller kids now!'

'– and I didn't even know there *were* black squirrels! So I bet no one else will have any photographs of them,' Orla was telling her dad excitedly as he raked up lawn cuttings the following day.

She loved the scent of freshly cut grass. It was a happy summery smell.

Mr Newton shook his head. 'I've never heard of it before either. I'd love to see them and I bet your mum would too. And Grace doesn't have to go to sports club today, so we could all come with you to see them. What?' he

stopped as Orla frowned and folded
her arms.

'How am I supposed to get any
photos with everyone galumphing
around the garden like fairy elephants
and upsetting the squirrels? And I
really I don't need Grace there handing
out advice! I'll just get all nervous
and drop the camera again. Like at
Borton Pits –' she stopped guiltily, but
luckily her dad didn't seem to have
noticed.

Mr Newton began cleaning the
mower. 'Hmm. I can see your point.
How about if I drop you off early,
and then we all come along a bit later
on?'

'Perfect!' Orla exclaimed.

Her mum came to tell them Sunday lunch was ready. Linking arms with her dad, Orla went into the house.

'Here you are, Flame. I've managed to get you some lunch.' Orla brought a small dish of meat and gravy into her bedroom.

But he wasn't napping on her bed
where she had left him.

'Where are you?' she asked, smiling.
'Oh, I get it! You're playing hide and
seek. Coming, ready or not!'

She put the dish down and then
looked for Flame under the bed, in the
wardrobe and behind the curtains. She
even pulled out the chest of drawers
and looked behind it. But there was
still no sign of him.

'Flame?' she called, beginning to feel
worried.

A very faint whimper came from
the bed. Orla noticed a tiny mound
in the duvet where it lay against the
pillows. She folded the duvet back
and saw Flame's fluffy brown tail

sticking out from beneath her pillow.

'What's wrong? Are you sick?' she asked, lifting the pillow and stroking him gently. She could feel Flame trembling all over and his chocolate-brown fur seemed dull.

He turned to her with troubled green eyes. 'I can sense my enemies. They are very close,' he whined in terror.

Orla bit back a gasp. She had been dreading this moment and now it was here. Flame was in terrible danger. Maybe Flame could still stay with her if she could find a way to help him.

'I won't let those horrible spies get you! What about hiding in our garage? Or I can take you to my aunt and uncle and you can hide in their garden for a few days —'

'No, Orla. It is too late,' Flame interrupted with an urgent little mew. 'If I stay completely still my enemies may pass by. Just leave me alone for a little while, please.'

'Well . . . OK then,' Orla said in a small voice.

Very gently, she tucked the pillow and duvet round Flame's tiny form so he was completely hidden again. She really hated to think of losing her friend, but she knew she was going to have to be strong and do as Flame asked.

'Orla! Are you ready yet? Dad's getting the car out!' Grace called impatiently up the stairs.

'Just coming!' Orla answered.

As she grabbed her bag and went
downstairs, Orla felt her throat tighten
with sadness. She hoped like mad that
Flame would still be here when she got
back from her aunt and uncle's house.

Chapter
★ EIGHT ★

Orla crouched behind the flowering bush in her aunt and uncle's garden. She had a clear view of the squirrel feeding station.

But although she was trying to feel excited about seeing the black squirrels again, her worries about Flame kept pushing into her mind.

As a faint rustle came from a nearby flower bed, Orla forced herself to concentrate. She checked that the camera was ready. This time, she wasn't going to mess it up.

A clump of leaves in the flower bed shook as something ran past them. Orla held her breath, ready to take a photo at the first sight of the squirrels.

Here they came!

Orla pressed the button. But instead of a black squirrel, a cute brown nose dusted with yellow pollen appeared followed by two bright emerald eyes and a pair of pointed chocolate-brown ears. The tiny kitten sprang out of the marigolds and landed on the lawn in a single bound.

'Flame!'

Orla only just managed to stop herself from laughing out loud with joy and relief as he ran over to her. 'You're still here! And I've just taken your photo!'

Flame rubbed himself against her ankles, purring loudly. 'My enemies have passed by, but they still might come back. If they do I will have to leave at once.'

Behind the bush, Orla picked Flame up and cuddled him. She was so pleased to see him again that she couldn't quite take it in. She just hoped his enemies kept passing by forever.

'I could have sworn the squirrels were in that flower bed,' Orla heard her uncle saying.

'They can't have been. Here they are
now, coming through the plum tree,'
her aunt replied softly.

Flame jumped down and Orla quickly
pointed the camera. The squirrels ran
down the plum tree's trunk on to the
lawn and headed for the feeding station.

Click! Orla took a photo as they

scrambled across a rope. Click! She took another as one of them sat on top of a pole holding a peanut in its delicate paws. Click! Click! She took more shots just as one of the squirrels jumped right into the air, its bushy tail flying straight out behind it.

'I've really got the hang of the camera now!' she whispered to Flame.

The squirrels leapt and ran and jumped about on the feeding station for another five minutes. Finally they each grabbed a fat peanut and wove and climbed their way back down on to the lawn.

Orla kept taking photos, until the squirrels ran back into the plum tree and disappeared over the garden fence.

'That was amazing,' Orla said to

Flame. 'If I haven't got some good stuff this time I'll eat Grace's smelly trainers!' When Flame looked startled, she laughed. 'Only kidding!'

Orla felt nervous, but excited as her dad drove towards the community centre a week later.

'Fancy one of your photos being picked,' Mr Newton said proudly. 'I can't wait to see it displayed with the rest of the shortlist.'

'I know. I can't believe it,' Orla said.

'Me neither. It's a complete miracle,' Grace murmured.

Orla grinned to herself. Even Grace couldn't dampen her spirits today!

Inside the community centre, Orla

walked round, holding Flame in her
shoulder bag.

Crowds of people moved about,
looking at the display boards. Orla saw
Joe with his parents. He came over to
her.

'Your photo's amazing. It should definitely win,' Joe said.

'Thanks. It's not bad, is it?' Orla said modestly.

It was the photo of the black squirrel in mid-air. Every detail of its glossy black coat, alert face and bushy tail was clearly detailed and in perfect focus. Properly mounted on black board and with a white border it looked very professional.

'Good luck, Orla.' Her aunt and uncle came over to give her a hug.

'Thanks,' she said, beaming.

The lady mayor in a smart purple suit and a thick gold chain was doing the judging. Orla held her breath as the mayor walked round, pausing now and then to examine a photo.

She was coming over! Orla held her breath. The mayor stopped and put a yellow sticker on the photo next to hers.

'What's a yellow sticker mean?' she asked Joe, as the mayor moved on.

'I think that's third prize. A blue sticker is second and red is first,' he replied.

The mayor stopped and looked at Orla's photo, before moving slowly past.

'I guess that's it then,' Orla said, trying not to feel too disappointed. 'It's hot in here. I'm going outside for a minute. I'll see you later.'

'I do not think that the judging is over yet,' Flame mewed as Orla moved down a long corridor towards the exit. There were lots of rooms on either side.

'You're not going to do anything magical, are you? Remember what I said about cheating?' Orla said.

'I remem—' Flame's purr ended abruptly.

Orla frowned in surprise and put out her hand to stroke him, but her fingers closed on empty space. She was just in time to glimpse the tiny brown kitten streaking through a nearby door that stood ajar. A notice on the door read 'Storeroom'.

Suddenly Orla glimpsed fierce, shadowy cat shapes. They were peering into all the rooms.

Flame's enemies had found him!

Orla's heart missed a beat. Without a second thought she hurried into the storeroom to warn Flame.

A bright white flash blinded her for a second. Orla blinked hard and then saw a regal young white lion standing in front of some stacked chairs. Thousands of tiny jewel-like sparks glittered in his glossy coat.

Prince Flame! He was no longer in disguise as a fluffy chocolate-brown kitten. Orla had forgotten how magnificent Flame looked as his true self.

An older-looking grey lion with a kind wise face stood beside Flame. 'We must leave now,' he rumbled.

'Goodbye, Flame. I'll never forget

you,' Orla said, her voice catching in
her throat.

Prince Flame nodded sadly. 'You have
been a good friend, Orla.'

Orla blinked away tears. Rushing
forward she threw her arms round his
neck.

Prince Flame allowed her to give him one last cuddle and then he took a step back. 'Be well, Orla. Be strong,' he said in a deep, velvety roar.

As Orla waved, there was a final spurt of bright silvery sparks that hung in the air for a moment before dissolving. Both big cats began to fade and then they were gone.

Orla heard a growl of rage. She turned to see the dark cat shapes slinking through the doorway and then they too disappeared.

Orla stood there, her heart aching. She was relieved that Flame was safe, but she was going to miss him terribly.

Slipping her hand into her jeans

pocket, she took out the photo she had taken of Flame jumping out of her aunt and uncle's flower bed. There was nothing there, except a faint sparkly blurred shape of a young lion. To anyone else it looked like a trick of the light.

But Orla knew it was Flame.

She would always have this reminder of the time she had shared with the tiny magic kitten.

'Orla? Where are you?' called Joe's voice. He grabbed her arm as she came out of the storeroom. 'You've won! Come and see. The mayor's just put a red sticker on your photo!'

'Really?' Orla wiped her eyes and hurried after Joe.

As she slipped the precious photo back into her pocket, she felt herself beginning to smile.

Magic Kitten

A Summer Spell
9780141320144

Classroom Chaos
9780141320151

Star Dreams
9780141320168

Double Trouble
9780141320175

Moonlight Mischief
9780141321530

A Circus Wish
9780141321547

Sparkling Steps
9780141321554

A Glittering Gallop
9780141321561

Seaside Mystery
9780141321981

Firelight Friends
9780141321998

A Shimmering Splash
9780141322001

A Puzzle of Paws
9780141322018

Magic

Kitten

A Christmas Surprise
9780141323237

Picture Perfect
9780141323480

A Splash of Forever
9780141323497

Magic Kitten

A Splash of Forever

Flame needs to find a purrfect new friend!

And that's how brave Alice faces her fear of swimming when special grey and white kitten Flame arrives to make a real splash in her life . . .

Win a Magic Kitten goody bag!

An urgent and secret message has been left for Flame
from his own world, where his evil uncle is
still hunting for him.

Four words from the message can be found in
royal lion crowns hidden in *Picture Perfect*
Find the hidden words and put them together to complete
the message. Send it in to us and each month we will
put every correct message in a draw and pick out one lucky
winner who will receive a purrfect Magic Kitten gift!

Send your secret message, name and address on a postcard to:
Magic Kitten Competition
Puffin Books
80 Strand
London WC2R 0RL

Hurry, Flame needs your help!

Good luck!

n.co.uk

Visit:
penguin.co.uk/static/cs/uk/0/competition/terms.html
for full terms and conditions

Magic Puppy

A New Beginning
9780141323503

Muddy Paws
9780141323510

Cloud Capers
9780141323527

Star of the Show
9780141323534

puffin.co.uk